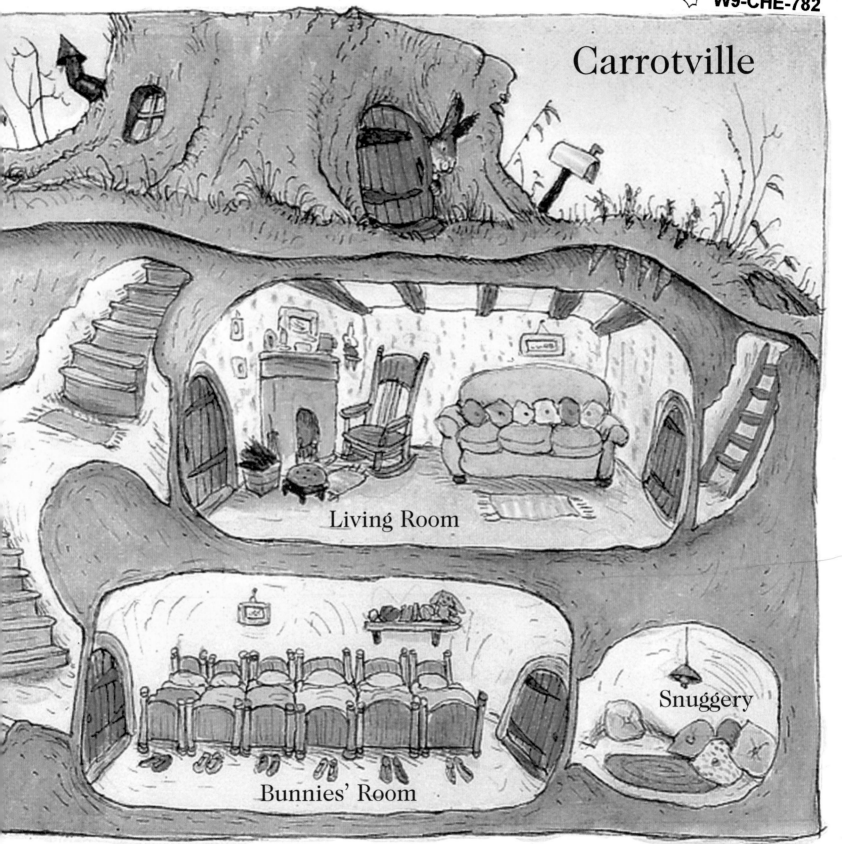

Carrotville

Living Room

Bunnies' Room

Snuggery

Bunny Tails

By Barbara Brenner, William H. Hooks and Betty Boegehold

Illustrated by Lynn Munsinger

MILK & COOKIES PRESS™

New York

Distributed by Simon & Schuster, Inc.

Rhoda, Rena, Ricky, Rooter, Rowdy, and Margaret Rose were heading for home.

"I'm starving," said Rhoda. "I hope Mama made something good for dinner."

The six little rabbits scampered down the rabbit hole. But when they hopped into the kitchen, there was no welcome smell of cooking. There was only a note on the table. It said:

"Dear Children: Grandma Rabbit has the flu and I am hopping off to see her. You will have to make your own dinner. I'm sure that together you can cook something good."

Rhoda Rabbit groaned.

"No dinner! And I'm starving!" She thumped one paw on the floor impatiently.

Ricky said, "I know how to make soup. Let's get started."

"Count me out. I'm too hungry to help," said Rhoda.

Ricky filled the big pot with water and put it on the stove.
He added a pinch of salt and a dash of pepper.

"Now that's a good start," he said.

"Start for what?" asked Rhoda.

"For delicious soup," said Ricky.

"It doesn't look like soup," said Rhoda. "It looks like water."

"There is one thing it needs," said Ricky. "Every good soup needs a potato."

Rena pricked up her ears. She remembered the potato she was saving under her bed for a rainy day. "If all it needs is a potato, I know where to find one," she said.

Rena ran and got the potato. Ricky peeled it and sliced it and dropped it into the pot.

He stirred the soup and tasted it. "Now we're getting somewhere," he said.

"Is it soup yet?" asked Rhoda in a cranky voice.

"Not quite yet," said Ricky. "It needs one more thing. A carrot," he announced. "It can't be soup without a sweet, crunchy carrot."

Rowdy's nose twitched. He had a carrot hidden in the attic.
"If it really needs a carrot, I guess I could find one," he said.
Rowdy brought the carrot to Ricky, who scraped it and diced
it and dropped it into the pot.

"It's beginning to smell like soup," said Ricky.

"Yes, but is it soup? I can't eat the smell," snapped Rhoda.

"It's not quite soup yet," said Ricky. "Mama says soup should always have something green in it."

Rooter said, "I have some green beans in my backpack."

Soon Rooter's green beans were simmering in the pot with the carrot and potato.

"Ah, what a soup," said Ricky. But in the next breath he said, "Uh-oh! I forgot."

"Forgot what?" wailed Rhoda.

"Soup needs a turnip for luck. And I know just where to find one." He reached into his pocket. "I was saving this for a snack."

A few minutes went by.

"Now is it soup?" whined Rhoda.

"We're getting there," said Ricky.

"Mama always puts celery in soup," said Margaret Rose. "And I found some in the fridge."

"You're right, little sister," said Ricky. "Just what this soup needs."

"I think I just fainted from hunger," snarled Rhoda.

The soup smelled wonderful. The noses of the six rabbits twitched, and their tummies rumbled.

They watched anxiously as Ricky tasted one more time.

"Hmmm," he muttered. "It's close. But something is still missing."

"I don't believe this," groaned Rhoda. She grabbed the spoon from Ricky. "I'll taste it," she said.

Rhoda took a spoonful of soup.

She tasted Rena's potato . . . and she tasted Rowdy's carrot . . . Rooter's green beans . . . Ricky's turnip . . . Margaret Rose's celery. Yes, there *was* something missing.

Suddenly she knew what was missing. *She* was missing. She was the only one who hadn't helped with the soup!

"I know what it needs," she said. "This soup needs some parsley to sprinkle on top. And I know just where to find some."

Rhoda ran down to the snuggery. There was the pot of parsley she kept just for herself. She brought it back to the kitchen.

Snip, snip. She cut some fresh leaves of parsley into the soup. "There," she said. "Now it's soup."

And they all sat down to eat.

"That was the best soup I ever ate," said Ricky.

"The very best," said Rena.

"Hear, hear," said Rowdy.

"Is there a name for this kind of soup?" Rooter wanted to know.

Rhoda said, "I think we should call it Group Soup, because everyone helped to make it. Even a very hungry, cranky rabbit."

Rhoda Rabbit's ears twitched happily.

The next day, an old rabbit in a polka-dot jacket came hopping down the path to Carrotville.

Who'll buy my ribbons bright?
Blue, red, or snowy white?
Rainbow ribbons, purple, pink, or green?
The prettiest ribbons you've ever seen!

"It's Ribbon Rabbit! He's here!" called Rhoda.

All the rabbits rushed out to take a look at Ribbon Rabbit's wares.

Rowdy, Ricky, and Rooter looked at the ribbons. "Just stuff for girls," said Rowdy.

"Oh, Mama," cried Rhoda, Rena and Margaret Rose. "Let us buy some ribbons!"

"Please let us," begged Rena.

"Hold your carrots," said Mama Rabbit. "I'll buy you some ribbons."

"Me first," yelled Rhoda.

"No, *me* first," said Rena.

"No, no, *me* first," cried Margaret Rose.

"Great jumping gerbils!" shouted Mama Rabbit. "Quiet! You can choose in alphabetical order!"

Margaret Rose bounced up and down. "*M* for Margaret Rose comes before *R* for Rena and Rhoda!" she cried. "So, I'm the first to choose. And I choose red!"

Ribbon Rabbit pulled out a shiny ribbon, red as lips, red as fire, red as a rose. "Rosy red for Margaret Rose," he said.

"That's me!" shouted Margaret Rose. "I always choose red. Red as a rose, for Margaret Rose!"

"Me next," said Rena, "because *Re* comes before *Rh*. I choose blue."
Ribbon Rabbit flipped out another shiny ribbon, blue as the sea,
blue as a baby's eyes. "Blue for a bunny named Rena," he said.

"I'm last," said Rhoda,
"but I'll pick the best
ribbon of all. I choose this
rainbow ribbon that's
green, yellow, orange, red,
purple, and blue."

Ribbon Rabbit held
up a shiny, shimmering
ribbon and said, "A
rainbow ribbon for
Rhoda Rabbit."

Margaret Rose stopped
chanting. She frowned. "I
want the rainbow ribbon,"
she shouted.

"Too bad. It's mine," said Rhoda.

"Not fair! I didn't see it,"
said Margaret Rose. "I'm
taking the rainbow ribbon."

"Oh, no, you aren't," shouted Rhoda.

Margaret Rose began to cry. "It's not fair," she sobbed. "I won't live here anymore if you are all so mean to me."

"No more about ribbons," said Mama Rabbit. "Come on Ribbon Rabbit, let's have lunch. Soup's on, everybody."

All the bunnies ran to the kitchen. All except Margaret Rose. She stopped crying.

She said, "They're so mean to me. If I'd seen that rainbow ribbon first, I would have picked it. It's really mine, so I'll go and take it."

Tippy-hop-tippy-hop, Margaret Rose stole into the living room, where the rainbow ribbon was lying on a chair. She put down her ribbon, and picked up the rainbow one and stuffed it in her pocket. Then, she went to the kitchen for soup.

Soon all the soup was gone and Ribbon Rabbit hopped on down the road.

Rhoda and Rena went to get their ribbons. Rhoda screamed, "Somebody stole my ribbon!"

Mama Rabbit rushed into the room.

"Mean, rotten Margaret Rose stole my ribbon and left me her red one," sobbed Rhoda.

"Don't call your sister mean and rotten," said Mama. "What did you do with the rainbow ribbon?" she asked Margaret Rose.

"It's my ribbon," said Margaret Rose. "I'm not going to stay here. I'm going away forever!"

She thumped out of the house and down the road. But pretty soon, she began to feel lonesome. Margaret Rose didn't like being alone, especially outside the house.

She sat down on the grass. The rainbow ribbon felt heavy in her pocket.

Someone sat down beside her. It was Ribbon Rabbit. "I'll give you all my ribbons, if you give me something," he said.

"What can I give you?" asked Margaret Rose.

"Your family," said Ribbon Rabbit. "You are going away forever, aren't you? And you like ribbons better than your family, right? I have no family, so it's a fair trade. Right?"

Margaret Rose's lip began to quiver. A big tear ran down her cheek.
"I do like my family," she sobbed. "I like them better than ribbons.
I'll give Rhoda her ribbon. I want to go home."

Margaret Rose stood up. "I know!" she said. "You come home with me,
too. Then, we'll both have a family!"

"Leaping lettuce leaves!" cried Ribbon Rabbit.
"What a terrific idea!"
So paw in paw, Margaret Rose and Ribbon Rabbit
hopped home together singing:
Rainbow ribbons, purple, pink, or green,
the prettiest ribbons you've ever seen!

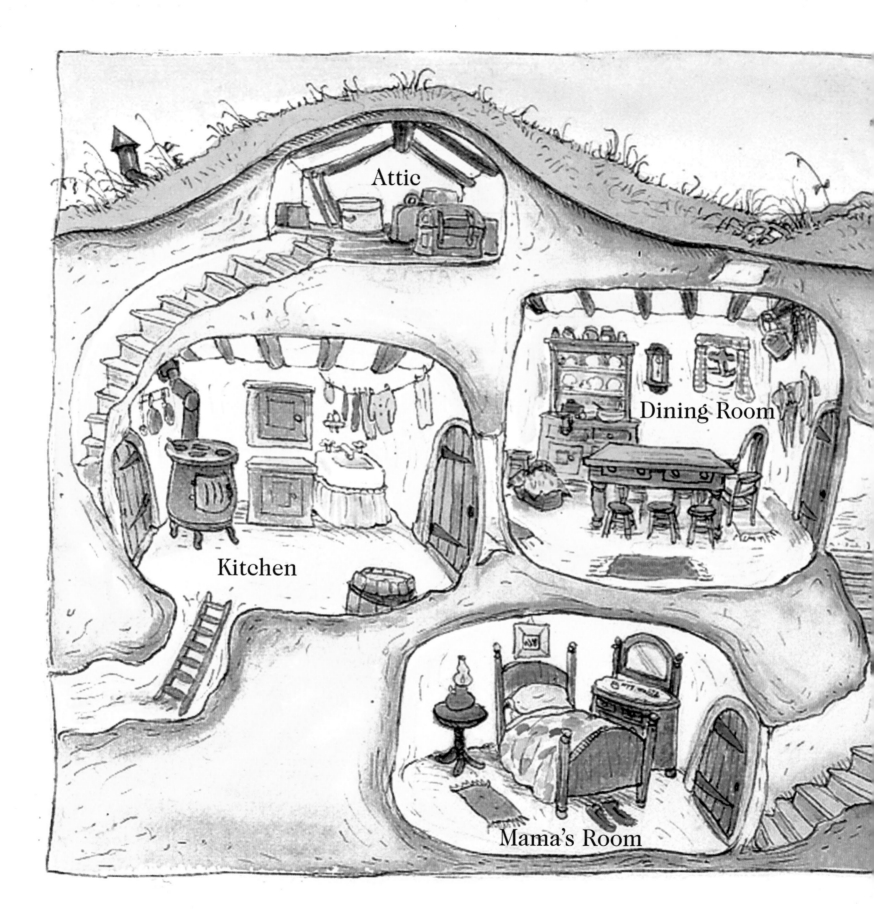